Nancy Drew and the Clue Crew™

#14

The Zoo Crew

By Carolyn Keene

Illustrated by Macky Pamintuan

Aladdin Paperbacks
New York London Toronto Sydney

P9-BYC-171

🐿 ALADDIN PAPERBACKS

An imprint of Simon & Schuster Children's Publishing Division

1230 Avenue of the Americas, New York, NY 10020

Text copyright © 2008 by Simon & Schuster, Inc.

Illustrations copyright © 2008 by Macky Pamintuan

All rights reserved, including the right of reproduction in whole or in part in any form.

NANCY DREW AND THE CLUE CREW is a trademark of Simon & Schuster, Inc.

NANCY DREW, ALADDIN PAPERBACKS, and related logo are registered trademarks of Simon & Schuster, Inc.

Designed by Lisa Vega

The text of this book was set in ITC Stone Informal.

Manufactured in the United States of America

First Aladdin Paperbacks edition May 2008

10 9 8

Library of Congress Control Number 2007934381

ISBN-13: 978-1-4169-5899-4

ISBN-10: 1-4169-5899-1

0316 OFF

CONTENTS

CHAPTER ONE

Monkey Business

"I wonder what our first day at zoo camp will be like," said Nancy Drew, smiling at her two best friends.

"I heard we earn junior zookeeper badges," Bess Marvin said excitedly. "If we do a good job!"

"I heard they put real bugs in the bug juice," George Fayne said.

Nancy and Bess stared at George.

"Quit it, George," said Bess. "You know I hate bugs and snakes more than you hate your real name—"

"Don't say it!" George cut in.

"Too late!" Bess said. She pointed to the

1

stick-on label on George's camp T-shirt. "It's on your name tag."

George looked down and groaned. There it was in big red letters: GEORGIA FAYNE!

Nancy giggled as George turned her name tag upside down. It was summer vacation, and River Heights Zoo Camp would be a blast. For the next three days the girls would learn about animals, make animal crafts, and work with zookeepers.

More campers filed into the building. Nancy thought they looked around eight years old, the same age as Bess, George, and herself.

Nancy also recognized one camper from her third-grade class at River Heights Elementary School. Kevin Garcia smiled as he walked over.

"What are you guys doing at zoo camp?" he asked. "I thought you'd be at a special mystery camp for detectives!"

Nancy, Bess, and George traded smiles. They loved solving mysteries. They even had their own detective club they called the Clue Crew.

But they loved something else just as much.

"We love animals," Nancy told Kevin. She straightened her zoo camp cap over her reddish blond hair. "And that's no mystery!"

A young woman dressed in a dark green jumpsuit clapped her hands three times for attention.

"I'm your counselor, Joanne Menendez," she said with a smile. "I'm also a zookeeper here at the zoo."

"A real live zookeeper," Bess whispered. "How cool is that?"

"We're in the Discovery Den," Joanne said, pointing around the room. "There are no animals in here, but there is all kinds of information about animals."

Nancy caught George smiling at a computer. George was a computer whiz and proud of it. She had wanted to go to computer camp—until she heard the food was yucky!

"We'll roll out our sleeping bags in here at night," Joanne went on. "But for now, why don't you find some empty cubbies and unpack your gear?"

The kids dragged their gear to the cubby shelves. Nancy, Bess, and George picked cubbies next to each other.

"Why did you bring so many clothes, Bess?" asked George. "We're going to be wearing our camp T-shirts!"

"Some of my blouses look great over T-shirts," Bess said. "And I couldn't decide which shorts to bring, so I brought all seven pairs!"

"What did you pack, George?" Nancy asked.

"Whatever was clean," George said with a shrug.

Bess and George were cousins, but they were as different as giraffes and elephants. Bess had blond hair and blue eyes and a closet full of cool clothes. George had dark hair and eyes— and a closet full of worn-out sneakers!

A girl with short brown hair and freckles walked over to the Clue Crew. Nancy glanced at her name tag: Abby Warner. Without saying hi, Abby dumped her pink duffel bag on the floor.

"Pink is my favorite color," Bess noted.

"It's not pink," said Abby. "It's dusty rose."

"If it's dusty, you'd better clean it," George joked.

"Cute," Abby groaned under her breath. She quickly stacked her clothes into her cubby. Then she slid her empty duffel bag under the shelf and huffed away.

"Snooty alert, snooty alert," whispered George.

When all the bags were unpacked, the kids sat on the floor around Joanne. Nancy read her fellow campers' name tags one by one: Brian Vance, Antonio Ramos, Marnie Patakis, Vinnie Porchnik, Abby, and Kevin.

"Okay!" Joanne announced. "Who's ready to get up close and personal with the animals?"

All hands shot up—except Bess's.

"As long as it's not snakes," she said with a shudder. "They give me goose bumps on my goose bumps."

"That's wimpy!" Brian scoffed. "Snakes are awesome!"

He and Antonio shared a high five.

"I like snakes too," said Vinnie. He popped a gummy worm into his mouth. "If they're the candy kind!"

"All of our snakes are behind glass in the snake house," Joanne explained. "But before we meet any of the animals, I want you all to split up into three teams."

George did the math in her head. "Nine kids total equals three kids on each team," she figured out.

"One, two, three!" Bess said, pointing her finger at Nancy, George, and herself.

After the teams were picked, the campers picked zoo-cool team names. Nancy, Bess, and George became Team Panda. Kevin, Marnie, and Vinnie were Team Rhino. Abby, Brian, and Antonio were Team Weasel.

Joanne explained the purpose of the teams. Each day they would take turns doing a different zoo job, like making snacks for the animals, tidying the petting zoo, and building enrichment toys.

"Enrichment toys are toys that animals can learn from," Joanne told the campers. "They learn how to use their claws, how to find food, or just have fun."

"Can Team Rhino make the animal snacks?" Kevin asked. "I won an ice-cream-making contest once."

"I won an ice-cream-*eating* contest!" Vinnie put in.

"Okay!" Joanne agreed with a smile.

"Making toys sounds cool," said Abby.

Bess hopped up and down excitedly. "Can Team Panda make toys, Joanne?" she asked. "I like to build things!"

"Wait a minute!" Abby said. "I asked first!"

"All teams will get a chance at each job," said Joanne. "Today Team Panda will make the enrichment toys."

"Phooey!" Abby muttered. "Now we have to clean the stinky petting zoo."

"Thanks to Team Panda," Brian added.

Bess shrugged at Nancy as if to say, *What did I do?*

Just then, the door flew open and a man stepped in. He wore a River Heights Zoo Camp T-shirt and checkered pants.

"Is everybody having fun?" he boomed.

"Kids, this is Ron Furbisher, the owner of the River Heights Zoo," Joanne said.

"Congratulations, everyone!" said Ron. "As campers you will all be part of the zoo's special Project Wildebeest!"

"What's that?" Vinnie asked.

"Glad you asked!" Ron replied cheerily. "For the next three days, each zoo animal will get the same amount of food and toys."

"How come?" wondered Abby.

"It's important to keep their daily routines the same," Ron explained. "So the scientists can study their behavior."

"Are *we* making the toys and snacks for Project Wildebeest?" Nancy asked.

"You bet!" exclaimed Ron. "That's why Project

Wildebeest and the zoo are counting on you!"

Excited whispers filled the room.

Ron rubbed his hands together and smiled. "Now that you know all about Project Wildebeest," he said, "how about a private tour of the zoo?"

"Yes!" Bess cheered, hopping up and down.

When the campers left the Discovery Den, they saw that the zoo was packed with visitors. Kids held balloons shaped like birds and animals. Carts sold stuffed animals and snacks. Vinnie stopped to buy a bag of bright yellow cotton candy.

"If you own the zoo, do you live here too?" Kevin asked Ron.

"You bet!" Ron said.

"In a cage?" gasped Antonio.

"We live in a *house* at the zoo." Ron chuckled. "Besides, there are no cages here. Just natural habitats."

"Heads up, you guys!" a voice yelled out.

Everyone turned to see a kid hopping over on

some weird-looking fuzzy animal feet. The boy knocked right into Antonio, sending him crashing to the ground.

"Sorry," the boy said. "I was trying out my new invention—Ethan Furbisher's Totally Neat Kangaroo Feet!"

Ethan lifted one foot to show what he meant. Underneath the fuzzy slipper was a row of springs.

"The zookeepers can wear them to keep up with the kangaroos," Ethan explained. "Am I brilliant or what?"

"This is my son, Ethan," Ron told the campers. "He's nine years old and wants to be an inventor when he grows up."

"I'm already an inventor, Dad!" Ethan said as he hopped up and down. "See? They work! They work! They work!"

Ethan seemed to lose control of his feet as he

began hopping away. "Whooooaaaaaa!" he cried.

"I guess he forgot to invent brakes," said Vinnie.

Ron continued the tour. The kids met giraffes, hippos, and lions. Bess kept her eyes closed in the Snake House, but she loved the Butterfly House.

"Now for a special surprise," Ron said. He pointed to a gray brick building. "Welcome to the Chimp Compound!"

"As in chimpanzees?" asked Nancy excitedly.

"You don't see that at computer camp!" George exclaimed.

Once inside, the campers were greeted by a woman wearing a white lab coat. She introduced herself as Petula Woodruff. Petula said she had studied chimpanzees in the jungle for many years.

"Petula is now doing her own study here at the zoo," said Ron. "It's called Project Primate."

"Yes," Petula said with a smile. "I'm teaching

chimpanzees human skills. Like how to make their own beds, sweep the floor, even how to lock and unlock doors."

"What for?" Brian asked.

"To see how smart chimpanzees can be," Petula replied.

"In that case," Vinnie joked, "can you teach them to do my homework? Yuk, yuk."

Petula stared at the cotton candy in Vinnie's fist. "No feeding the chimpanzees, please," she said nervously.

Then Petula led the campers into a small room. Everyone smiled when they saw chimpanzees setting a table. Another chimp followed, placing a banana on each plate.

"As you can see, the chimps in the compound have perfect manners," Petula said. "If they could talk, they would probably say please, thank you, excuse me—"

Clunk! One chimp dropped a plastic dish. It rolled over to Kevin, and he picked it up.

"Catch!" Kevin tossed the dish like a Frisbee.

The chimp caught it between long fingers. But instead of placing it on the table, he began screeching and jumping.

Soon all the chimps went wild, tossing their plates around the room. Nancy ducked to avoid a flying dish.

"It's a chimp attack!" shouted Brian. "Chimp attaaaaaack!"

ChaPTER TWO

Creaky and Freaky!

"Stop, please!" Petula told the chimps. She pursed her lips and began to hoot. "Hoo-hoo-hooooooo!"

The chimps froze.

"How'd you do that?" Nancy asked Petula.

"I spoke chimp language," Petula explained. "I told them that tossing dishes is unsafe and not a part of Project Primate."

The kids stared at Petula. *All that in three hoots?* Nancy thought.

"Maybe they just want to play," said Bess.

"The chimps *do* play," Petula said with a smile. "With special educational games from our development laboratory."

Nancy was glad when the tour of the Chimp Compound was over. "Too much monkey business," she said.

"Chimps aren't monkeys," Marnie pointed out. "They're apes."

"How did you know that?" asked Nancy.

"I want to be a veterinarian when I grow up," Marnie said proudly. "I read every book about animals I can find."

Outside, Marnie ran over to Ron. "Can we see the animal hospital here at the zoo, Mr. Furbisher?" she asked.

"You'll all get a tour of the animal hospital tomorrow," Ron answered.

"Tomorrow?" Marnie said softly. "I can't wait."

"Hey, you guys!" Antonio piped up. "I think I just heard a tiger growl!"

"That was my stomach," Vinnie said, patting his belly. "It must be time for lunch."

Vinnie was right. The kids ate lunch in the zoo cafeteria. Bess was glad there was no bug juice—or bugs!

After lunch Nancy, Bess, and George ran to the Animal Arts Center to make enrichment toys. Their instructor was a friendly zookeeper named Tim.

"Check out some enrichment toys," Tim said, pointing to a table. "As you see, they don't run on batteries!"

The three friends looked at the toys. There were painted cardboard tubes for ferrets to crawl through and knotted ropes for the rabbits. Even a pail filled with dirt and ants for meerkats to dig through.

"We'll make one toy for each animal," Tim said. He held up a list of the zoo animals. "Those are the Project Wildebeest rules."

The girls sat down at the worktable. Tim showed them how to tie knots in pieces of rope for the rabbits to play with. Nancy was about to try one when Ethan raced through the door.

"Yo, Tim, look at the new toy I invented!" he cried. He held up a burlap sack tied together at the top. "I call it Ethan's Party Animal Peanut Piñata!"

"Peanut piñata?" Nancy giggled.

"For the elephants!" Ethan explained. "They hold a stick in their trunks and whack it until it's peanuts all around!"

"Thanks for sharing, Ethan," Tim said. "But Nancy, Bess, and George were about to make rope toys for the rabbits."

"Big deal!" Ethan said. "I made a rope toy for the rabbits too. But mine has a carrot tied to the end of it!"

"Do the animals play with your toys?" asked Bess.

"No," Ethan grumbled. "My dad thinks my toys are silly."

Ethan flung his peanut piñata over his shoulder. Then he turned and walked out the door.

"That Ethan!" Tim chuckled. "He'll do anything to make toys for the animals."

After making rabbit toys, the girls made feather dusters for the parrots to play with.

They painted rubber balls for the seals to bounce in their pond. When they were done, it was time to give their toys to the animals.

Nancy pulled a writing pad from her waist pack. It was decorated with penguins—perfect for zoo camp!

"I'm going to keep track of every toy we give to the animals," Nancy said, "as part of Project Wildebeest."

"Good idea," Tim told her. "Why don't we start with the rabbits in the petting zoo?"

The visitors had all gone home by the time the girls entered the petting zoo. As Nancy looked around, she saw baby animals frolicking around mini cottages, tiny castles—even a windmill.

"This place is neat!" Nancy exclaimed.

"That's what you think!" a girl's voice grumbled.

Nancy turned to see Abby, Brian, and Antonio raking hay outside the llama pen.

"Wait till you have to clean the petting zoo,

Team Panda!" Abby said, wrinkling her nose.
"It's gross!"

One llama blew a gob of spit over the fence.
It landed with a splat on Abby's arm!

"Ewwww!" Abby screamed. "He got me! He
got me!"

"Drama queen," George whispered.

While Tim tried to calm Abby, the girls found

the rabbit hutch. It looked like a tiny white cottage. Inside were five adorable bunnies.

George opened the basket and pulled out five rope toys. Bess carefully laid them inside the rabbit hutch.

"Five bunnies—five toys," Nancy said, writing in her penguin pad. "Check."

The girls delivered the rest of the toys to the animals. Some were placed in cabinets outside the pens and habitats.

"Mission accomplished, Team Panda!" said Nancy as she shut her penguin pad.

That night the campers were treated to a yummy barbecue supper right in the zoo. Somewhere between the veggie burgers, potato salad, and dessert, a man dressed in a blue uniform walked over with a smile.

"Mind if I grab a brownie?" he asked.

"Kids, this is Cliff," Joanne explained. "He's the night watchman at the zoo."

"Are you the only one who works here at night?" Kevin asked.

Cliff shook his head. "The vets at the zoo hospital work nights," he said. "So do the zookeepers who take care of the nocturnal animals."

"Noc-what?" asked George.

"Nocturnal animals come out at night," Joanne explained. "They spend most of the night hunting for food."

Cliff held up a brownie. "Just like me!" he said.

The first busy day of camp came to an end when the campers unrolled their sleeping bags in the Discovery Den.

"Are you homesick?" Bess whispered in the dark.

"Not really," George whispered back. "Three days of camp is kind of like three sleepovers in a row."

Nancy thought so too. But she missed her dad and Hannah Gruen just a bit.

To Nancy, Mr. Drew was the best dad in the world. Hannah was the Drews' housekeeper. She'd been helping out Nancy's dad since Nancy was three years old. That was when Nancy's mother died. Hannah could never take the place of Nancy's mom, but with her hugs and choco-late chip cookies, she came pretty close.

The voices of the other campers began drop-ping off one by one. Soon everyone but Nancy was fast asleep.

I'll count sheep, Nancy thought as she closed her eyes. *One . . . two . . . three . . .*

Creak! Nancy's eyes popped open. She tried to see where the noise came from. It was too dark to see anything.

Lying perfectly still, Nancy listened for the noise again. When she didn't hear it, she guessed it was one of the animals outside.

This is *a zoo*, Nancy told herself sleepily. *Four . . . five . . .*

"Maybe you heard one of those nocturnal animals, Nancy," said Bess the next morning. "The kind that don't sleep at night."

"Maybe," Nancy said as she combed her hair in the girls' washroom.

George turned to Marnie, who was brushing her teeth at the next sink. "Watch out, Marnie!" she said. "You're dribbling toothpaste all over your T-shirt."

Marnie rinsed, spit—and yawned.

"Didn't you sleep last night, Marnie?" asked Nancy.

"Or are you nocturnal too?" Bess added, giggling.

"I can't sleep in a sleeping bag," Marnie said quickly. As she left the washroom, Joanne walked in.

"Hi, girls. I was just talking to some zoo-keepers," Joanne said seriously. "It looks like there weren't enough enrichment toys for some of the animals this morning."

Nancy, Bess, and George stared at Joanne.

"We counted the toys exactly, Joanne," said George.

"I kept track of them in my penguin pad!" Nancy said.

"I believe you." Joanne sighed. "But Ron won't be a happy camper when he finds out. This will set Project Wildebeest back a whole day."

The girls watched as Joanne left the wash-room.

"What if everybody blames us?" George asked. "Now we'll never get our zookeeper badges!"

"Forget the badges!" Bess said. "What about Project Wildebeest?"

"It's not our fault," Nancy insisted. "We gave

the right amount of toys to the animals."

"Then what happened to them?" Bess asked.

"They couldn't have disappeared," said Nancy. "Maybe somebody took the toys."

"Who?" Bess and George asked together.

"I don't know," Nancy said. "But we can try to find out."

"You mean solve a mystery?" Bess asked excitedly.

"Sure," Nancy replied with a smile. "We may be Team Panda—but we're also the Clue Crew!"

Chapter Three

Sneak Goes the Weasel

Bess couldn't wait to get started on the new case. But George wasn't so psyched.

"How can we solve a mystery at the zoo?" she asked. "We don't have our detective headquarters. And the computer in the Discovery Den just has animal facts."

Detective headquarters for the Clue Crew was in Nancy's bedroom at home. They used Nancy's computer for their case files and her desk drawer for their clues.

"I have an idea!" Nancy said. She pulled her penguin pad from the pocket of her hoodie. "We'll keep track of our suspects and clues in this!"

George stared at the pad and shrugged. "It doesn't have a keyboard or mouse." She sighed. "But I guess it'll do."

The girls sat cross-legged on the Discovery Den floor. Nancy opened her penguin pad to a fresh page. She wrote the word *Suspects* at the top.

"Who would want to steal enrichment toys from animals?" Nancy asked.

"Someone who doesn't like animals," suggested Bess.

"Or someone who doesn't like *us*!" George said.

"What do you mean?" asked Nancy.

"Team Weasel was in the petting zoo when we were giving our toys to the rabbits," George reminded her. "You saw how mad they were because we got the job they wanted."

"Maybe Team Weasel wanted to get even with us by stealing our toys," Bess said.

"And making us look bad!" added George.

Nancy wrote *Abby, Brian, and Antonio* on the page.

"We have our first suspects," she said. "But

we can't solve a mystery without clues."

"And I can't solve a mystery on an empty stomach," George declared, standing up. "Come on. Let's get breakfast!"

The girls changed from their pajamas to clean camp shirts and shorts. Then they ran to join the others on their way to the zoo cafeteria.

Marnie couldn't stop talking about the tour of the animal hospital they would take later.

"There's a whole room for baby animals in the hospital," she said excitedly. "They are so cute!"

"How do you know?" Vinnie asked.

Before Marnie could answer, Abby said in a loud voice, "Hey! Did you hear about the enrichment toys?"

"Hmm," said Antonio, rubbing his chin. "Didn't Nancy, Bess, and George make the toys yesterday?"

"Yup!" Brian said. "They may be detectives, but when it comes to counting—they don't have a clue!"

Team Weasel laughed as they ran ahead.

"Kevin must have told them we're detectives," Nancy said.

"And I'm telling Joanne that Team Weasel took those toys!" George said angrily. She began to run toward Joanne, but Nancy grabbed her arm.

"Wait, George!" said Nancy. "We can't accuse Team Weasel until we have some clues, remember?"

"Then let's go get some!" George said.

The girls slipped away from the others and raced to the petting zoo. It was early, so no visitors were inside, just a zookeeper feeding the goats. She didn't notice the girls as they scurried to the rabbit hutch.

George kneeled on the ground. A few bunnies scampered out of the little cottage as she stuck her head inside.

"What do you see, George?" Nancy asked.

"Rabbits, and just two of our rope toys." George's voice echoed inside the hutch. "Wait—what's this thing?"

George crawled out. In her hand was a piece of rope.

Attached to it was a carrot with bunny teeth marks.

"That's not our toy!" exclaimed Bess.

"And it wasn't here yesterday," George said. "Where'd it come from?"

Nancy studied the carrot on a rope. "You guys," she said slowly. "Didn't Ethan say he made a rabbit toy like that?"

"Yeah!" said George. "And didn't Tim say Ethan would do anything to make toys for the animals—"

"Nancy, Bess, George!" a voice cut in.

The girls whirled around. Joanne was standing outside the petting zoo with her hands on her hips.

"Please don't leave the group without asking me first," she said.

As the girls walked out of the petting zoo, Bess whispered to Nancy, "Do you think Ethan switched our toys with his own?"

"I'm not sure," Nancy answered. "But I am sure that Ethan Furbisher is our next suspect!"

CHAPTER FOUR

Snack . . . Attack!

Nancy, Bess, and George did not see Ethan or Team Weasel the rest of the morning. They were too busy with their new job of the day—making snacks for the animals in the zoo kitchen.

Barbara was the zoo's dietician. She taught the girls all about the foods animals ate. Some sounded pretty yummy, while others seemed gross!

"Pandas love to eat bamboo," Barbara said. "And reptiles eat mice. But don't worry, we won't be using that ingredient!"

"Thank goodness!" Bess sighed.

First the three girls helped Barbara make a

batch of cookies for the ponies. They mixed oatmeal, flour, shredded carrots, oil, and molasses. Then they rolled the dough into balls and lined them up on a cookie sheet.

While Barbara placed the cookies in the oven, the girls whipped up a fruit-and-nut mix for the parrots. After that they gathered bunches of grass for the zebras and poured milk into bottles for the baby goats and lambs.

"When do you think the toys were stolen?" Bess asked as they worked.

Nancy twisted a cap on a bottle. It made a squeaky noise, which made her remember the creaky noise she'd heard the night before.

Doors sometimes creak when they open and close, Nancy thought. *Maybe that's it!*

"I think the toys were stolen in the middle of the night," she declared.

"The middle of the night?" asked Bess.

Nancy nodded and then explained. "What if that noise I heard last night wasn't an animal?

What if it was someone sneaking out the door to steal the enrichment toys?"

"Like Team Weasel!" George said. She narrowed her eyes. "I'll bet they're as sneaky as their team name!"

"If Team Weasel did take our toys," Bess wondered, "where did they hide them?"

"The Discovery Den has tons of shelves and cubbies," said Nancy. "I wish we could search it while everybody is still at their zoo jobs."

"Me too," George said. "But how can we leave in the middle of our jobs?"

The girls finished filling the last baby bottles. Barbara looked up at the shelf and frowned.

"I ran out of baskets to put the bottles in," she said. "I'd go to the supply house to get more, but I can't leave the oven unattended."

"Where is the supply house?" Nancy asked.

"Not far," Barbara replied. "It's right behind the Discovery Den."

The Discovery Den?

"We'll get the baskets!" Nancy, Bess, and George said at the same time.

"All three of you?" Barbara asked.

"Buddy system!" said Nancy with a smile.

Barbara thought for a moment, then gave the girls permission to go to the supply house.

"Are we lucky or what?" George said as they hurried out of the zoo kitchen. "Now we can look for clues!"

But when they reached the Discovery Den, the door was locked. Nancy saw an open window, but it was too high to climb through.

"If only we were monkeys." Bess sighed. She nodded toward a tree by the window. "Then we could climb that tree and jump through the window."

"You don't have to be a monkey to climb a tree!" said George. She ran to the tree, grabbed a branch, and pulled herself up. Using her long legs, she scurried up the tree.

Nancy and Bess cheered as George slipped

through the open window. After a few seconds, the door flew open and George waved them inside.

"Good work, George," Nancy said. "Now let's look for those missing toys!"

The girls searched Team Weasel's cubbies. They found Brian's dirty socks, Abby's Very

Berry Shampoo, and Antonio's half-eaten granola bar—but no enrichment toys!

Nancy and George were about to look underneath the shelves when Bess called out, "Look at Abby's pink duffel bag!"

Nancy turned. The pink duffel bag was on the floor next to Abby's rolled-up sleeping bag. "What about it?" she asked.

"Abby emptied it the first day of camp, remember?" Bess said. "And now it looks totally stuffed!"

"Maybe Team Weasel put our enrichment toys in the bag," said George.

In a flash the girls were kneeling around Abby's duffel bag. Nancy grabbed the zipper. She began to unzip it.

BOOOOOOINGGG!!!!

The girls shrieked.

Leaping straight out of Abby's pink duffel bag was a giant snake!

CHAPTER FIVE

Fangs for Nothing

"Snaaaaaaaaake!!" Bess screamed.

The snake leaped out toward Nancy, Bess, and George. Still shrieking, the girls raced toward the open door. They were about to

charge out when they bumped into Team Weasel. Abby, Brian, and Antonio yelped as toys they were holding flew out of their hands.

"Hey! Watch where you're going!" said Antonio.

"Run!" George warned. "There's a big fat snake in Abby's bag!"

"What were you doing going through my bag?" Abby snapped. She huffed over to the snake curled on the floor.

"Omigosh—she's picking it up!" Bess squealed.

"Is she nuts?" cried George.

Nancy looked closer at the snake. It had a goofy face, purple fangs, and a price tag swinging from its tail!

"That snake is fake!" Nancy declared.

"His name is Fang," Abby said, swinging the snake proudly. "I bought him at the zoo gift shop before breakfast."

"We were going to stick Fang inside Bess's sleeping bag." Antonio laughed. "We know how much she hates snakes!"

"And I hate snakes in the grass," George said, glaring at Team Weasel.

Nancy looked at the toys Team Weasel had dropped. They looked just like the enrichment toys her team had made yesterday!

"Are those the missing toys you were bringing in here?" she demanded.

"Those are *our* toys!" said Abby. "Today's our day to make the enrichment toys, remember?"

"We were just going to give them to the animals," Antonio said. "When we saw you guys through the door, we wanted to see what was up."

Abby scowled at Nancy, Bess, and George.

"So that's why you were going through our stuff," Abby said. "You thought *we* stole the missing toys."

"Did you?" asked Bess.

Abby rolled her eyes. "For the Clue Crew, you're still pretty clueless," she answered. "We didn't take anything!"

"You just counted wrong," Antonio said.

"And you don't want to admit it."

"Come on, Team Weasel," said Brian. "Let's give the animals the toys we made. At least *we* know how to count!"

Abby tossed the stuffed snake at Bess. It fell on the floor as Bess jumped back.

Laughing, Team Weasel scooped up the toys. Then they made their way out the door.

"Weasels," George muttered.

"I knew it was fake all the time!" Bess said.

"Yeah, right," said Nancy. She picked up the snake and tossed it on Abby's duffel bag. But when she saw Abby's sleeping bag against the far wall, something clicked.

"You guys," Nancy said slowly, "Team Weasel slept way in the back of the room last night."

"So?" George asked.

"So they would have had to climb over the other sleeping bags to get to the door," Nancy pointed out. "They would have woken everybody up."

"Oh!" Bess said with wide eyes. "So whoever

sneaked out in the middle of the night was probably near the door."

"Team Rhino was sleeping near the door," George remembered. "But why would Kevin, Vinnie, or Marnie want to steal our toys?"

Nancy couldn't imagine Team Rhino stealing their toys. Vinnie and Marnie were so nice. And Kevin was their friend!

"I can't think of one reason," Nancy said.

The girls picked up some baskets from the supply house. Then they hurried back to the zoo kitchen. After packing up the snacks they made, it was time for the best part—feeding the animals!

Nancy, Bess, and George held the bottles as baby goats and lambs lapped at the milk. Ponies nibbled the carrot cookies, and parrots pecked at the dried fruits and nuts. Last but not least, the girls handed out bunches of grass to a few hungry zebras.

Nancy kept careful track of the snacks in her penguin pad. "Four zebras," she said as she wrote. "Four bunches of—"

"Ethan!" cried Bess.

"Four bunches of Ethan?" Nancy asked.

"No! There goes Ethan!" Bess said, pointing.

Nancy turned and saw Ethan. He was carrying a huge bag and darting through a crowd of visitors.

"He's still one of our suspects," Nancy reminded her friends. "We have to question him about the toys."

"Ethan!" George shouted. "Wait up!"

The girls ran through the zebra pen.

"Whoooooaaaaa!"

Nancy stopped running. She turned and saw George on the ground. Beneath her foot was a banana peel.

"Are you okay?" Nancy asked.

"I slipped on a mushy banana peel," said George, standing up. "Lucky for me, the ground was mushy too!"

"Since when do zebras eat bananas?" Bess asked.

"Maybe they get care packages," George joked. "This is camp, you know!"

The girls stepped out of the zebra pen. They were about to look for Ethan when Joanne called their names. It was time for the tour of the animal hospital.

"We'll find Ethan later," Nancy told her friends.

"He can't go too far," Bess pointed out. "He lives here."

The girls joined the others at the animal hospital. Once inside, a vet named Dr. Patel introduced the campers to Ambrose, a chimp from the compound. He sat on a table in the emergency room.

"What's wrong with him?" asked Marnie.

"Ambrose ate cotton candy," Dr. Patel explained. "It gave him a stomachache, but he seems to be feeling better now."

Ambrose grinned with blue-stained teeth.

Petula was in the office too. She spoke quietly to Joanne, but Nancy could hear her loud and clear.

"My chimps haven't left the compound in weeks," Petula said. "They have everything they need there."

"Then how did Ambrose get cotton candy?" asked Joanne.

"One of your campers was eating cotton candy during the tour," Petula said. "He probably gave Ambrose some."

"He didn't, Ms. Woodruff!" Nancy spoke up.

All eyes turned to Nancy.

"Vinnie was eating *yellow* cotton candy," Nancy explained. She pointed to Ambrose's teeth. "The cotton candy Ambrose ate was definitely blue."

"Hoo, hooo!" Ambrose hooted.

"Well . . . ," Petula said, "I suppose you're right."

Ambrose screeched as he hopped off the table. Everyone watched as he scampered to the door and twisted the handle.

"What is he doing?" asked Dr. Patel. "He can't leave until he gets his medicine."

Petula smiled as she ran for Ambrose. "The chimps in the compound learned how to open doors," she said. "Well done, Ambrose. Well done!"

Ambrose grinned, his teeth still blue from the cotton candy.

"I didn't think chimps liked cotton candy," said George. "I thought they ate mostly bananas and stuff."

"Bananas!" Bess said. Her eyes lit up. "Do you think maybe a chimp dropped that banana peel in the zebra pen?"

Nancy gave it a thought but shook her head. "What would chimps be doing in the zebra pen, even if they did go outside?" she asked.

"A field trip?" Bess guessed.

"Come on, campers!" Joanne called out. "Time to visit more animals."

The campers followed Joanne down a long hall.

"Are there any sick snakes here?" asked Brian.

"Yes," Marnie answered. "The reptile room is in the back of the hospital. They're in climate-controlled tanks."

Nancy blinked. Marnie sure knew a lot about animals. But how did she know so much about the animal hospital?

The rest of the tour was awesome. The campers watched an eagle having his broken wing x-rayed. They met a zebra with a sprained leg and even a hyena getting a tooth pulled.

Ron greeted the campers as they filed out of the zoo hospital. "Good work today, campers," he said. "But as you know, we had a little setback with the missing enrichment toys."

Nancy, Bess, and George glanced sideways at Team Weasel. Abby, Brian, and Antonio glanced sideways at them.

"Tomorrow is another day!" Ron boomed. "And with your can-do attitude, I know we can make Project Wildebeest work!"

The kids cheered and high-fived one another. Then everyone headed to the Discovery Den.

"Did you see the way Team Weasel looked at us?" Bess murmured.

"I don't care that their sleeping bags were in the back of the room," said George. "I think they did it!"

"There's still Ethan," Bess reminded her cousin. "If we could just find him."

Just then, Nancy saw Cliff. The night watchman was smiling as he entered the guard booth.

"Cliff was here all night," Nancy said. "Let's ask him if he knows anything about the missing toys!"

The girls ran to the booth. Nancy rapped on the door until Cliff opened it.

"Did you bring me some more brownies?" Cliff asked with a chuckle.

"No," Nancy admitted. "We just want to know if you heard or saw anything weird last night."

"Nope," said Cliff.

"Are you sure?" George asked.

"The zoo is real quiet at night," Cliff told the

girls. He pointed to a small TV on his desk. "So I always get to watch my spy shows!"

"Spy shows?" Nancy repeated.

"Do you girls like mysteries too?" asked Cliff.

"Totally!" Nancy giggled. She thanked Cliff and they walked away.

"Great," George muttered. "Cliff was too busy watching TV to see anything."

"What if the toynapper strikes again tonight?" Bess asked.

Nancy lowered her voice as they neared the Discovery Den. "Let's not sleep tonight," she suggested. "So if anyone tries to leave the Discovery Den, we'll catch him or her in the act!"

"You mean have a stakeout?" George asked.

"More like a stake-*in*," Nancy said. "If nocturnal animals can stay awake all night, so can we!"

Nancy's eyes opened to the sound of voices. She crawled out of her sleeping bag and tiptoed to the door. Looking outside, she saw it was morning. Glancing back, she saw Bess and George fast asleep!

Oh, no! Nancy thought. *We slept through the stakeout!*

Joanne, Ron, and a few zookeepers stood outside the Discovery Den. Their faces looked grim as they spoke to one another.

"Are you sure?" Joanne was saying.

"Sure I'm sure," one zookeeper replied. "The orangutans' toy cabinet was broken into last night. Most of their enrichment toys are gone."

Nancy gasped.

The toynapper had struck again!

ChaPTER Six

Gone in the Night

"Another snag for Project Wildebeest," groaned Ron. "The scientists will never be able to do their jobs!"

The other campers were still asleep as Nancy ran to Bess and George. She took turns shaking them awake.

"Bess, George," Nancy whispered.

"How's the stakeout going?" Bess mumbled.

"We slept through the stakeout!" Nancy hissed. "And more toys went missing last night!"

The two girls' eyes popped open as they jumped out of their sleeping bags. They followed Nancy to the door and peeked outside.

"Percy the parrot loved his new feather toy," the parrot handler was saying. "I think it reminded him of his mother!"

"Our boomer balls are gone too," the zookeeper in charge of large cats said. "Tula the tiger is not pleased!"

"Did Cliff see anything strange last night?" Joanne asked. "Did the nocturnal zookeepers see anything unusual?"

"The nocturnal zookeepers work inside," Ron said. "And Cliff said he didn't see a thing."

"Except his spy shows," George murmured.

Nancy nudged George with her elbow. She listened as Joanne asked, "What does this mean for Project Wildebeest?"

"I'll tell the scientists that I might call off Project Wildebeest." Ron sighed. "What good is it if we can't give the animals the same number of toys and snacks each day?"

Ron began walking away. Joanne and the zookeepers followed him, all talking at once.

"Team Weasel made the enrichment toys

yesterday," George whispered. "They wouldn't steal their own toys."

"If Team Weasel is innocent, that leaves Ethan," Bess reasoned. "Maybe we should tell Ron before he cancels Project Wildebeest."

"But we have only one clue that Ethan switched the toys," Nancy said. "The carrot on a rope!"

Nancy was about to get out her penguin pad when she heard a loud noise.

THUMP . . . THUMP . . . THUMP . . .

"What's that?" she whispered.

The girls stepped out of the Discovery Den. They followed the noise to the elephant pen. Inside, three elephants were standing around a tree. Their trunks were wrapped around sticks as they whacked at a hanging bag. Nancy recognized it at once.

"Ethan's peanut piñata!" she said.

"He did it again," said George. "He switched the enrichment toys with his own!"

"Come and get it, you guys!" a voice shouted.

The girls whirled around. Ethan was standing at the edge of the seal pond. He wore bright blue swim trunks and goggles. In his hands he held a gadget that was flipping rubber balls into the seal pond.

"There's Ethan," George said. "With another one of his inventions."

The girls ran to the seal pond.

"What do you think of my new Furbisher Flipper?" Ethan greeted them. "Am I brilliant or what?"

"Can we ask you some questions, Ethan?" asked Nancy.

"It depends." Ethan shrugged. "What kind of questions?"

"Like, did you take the animal enrichment toys we made and switch them with your own?" George blurted out.

"Why would I take anything here?" Ethan scoffed. "My mom and dad own the place."

"If that's true," Nancy said, folding her arms, "why are our toys missing, while your peanut piñata is swinging in the elephant pen?"

"Not to mention your carrot toy in the rabbit hutch," added Bess.

"Fess up, Furbisher!" George snapped.

"Okay, okay," Ethan said with a sly smile. "My answer is . . ."

He placed his Furbisher Flipper on the ledge.

Then he dropped into the seal pond with a splash.

Nancy, Bess, and George peered over the edge of the pond with wide eyes.

"Omigosh!" Nancy cried.

"Kid overboard!" shouted George. "Kid overboard!"

CHAPTER SEVEN

Clue in the Zoo

Nancy was about to run for help when Ethan crawled out of the water onto the rocks.

"Ethan, are you all right?" Nancy called.

"I jumped in myself," Ethan said with a laugh. "The water is super shallow. I swim in here all the time."

"Arp, arp arp!" barked a seal.

"Show-off!" Bess shouted. "You scared us half to death!"

The zookeeper wasn't happy either. "I don't care if you are the owner's son," he shouted. "No more swimming in the seal pond, Ethan!"

"Sorry," Ethan called. He jumped back in, swam to the ledge, and climbed out, dripping wet. "Okay, those *were* my toys."

Nancy stared at Ethan. "So you did switch our toys with yours?" she asked.

"I didn't have to!" Ethan exclaimed. "The zookeepers liked my toys. They took them from me, fair and square."

"They did?" Nancy asked.

"Yup!" said Ethan. "They don't think my toys are silly like my dad does!"

Ethan picked up his Furbisher Flipper. The seals barked as he walked away.

"Does the zoo gift shop sell lie detectors?" Bess asked.

Nancy heard one of the elephants trumpet in the distance. It gave her an idea.

"There's an easier way to see if Ethan is telling the truth," she said. "Follow me!"

In a flash the girls were back at the elephant pen. They could see the animals still whacking at the peanut piñata.

"Go for it, Mumbo," a zookeeper cheered. "Put some funk in your trunk!"

"Excuse me!" called Nancy. "Did you get that peanut piñata from Ethan Furbisher?"

"Sure did!" the zookeeper called back. "I know it's not part of Project Wildebeest, but the elephants love it!"

WHACK!

The peanut piñata burst open. Happy elephants trumpeted as a cascade of peanuts fell on the ground.

"Ethan's clean," Nancy said as they walked away.

"But those elephants need a bath!" said Bess. She squeezed her nose. "Pee-ew!"

By the time the campers ate breakfast they all knew about the missing toys.

"I can't believe it happened again," Kevin said. "I hope Ron doesn't call off Project Wildebeest."

"Me too!" said Abby. She turned to Nancy, Bess, and George. "If you're such great detectives, why can't you find out what happened to our toys?"

"We're working on it," George insisted. "Pass the strawberry jam!"

"Please," Bess added.

Nancy held her penguin pad on her lap as she secretly crossed off names on her suspect list: Abby, Brian, Antonio, and Ethan.

No more suspects, Nancy thought. *Zero. Zip. Zilch.*

"As you know, kids, tonight is the last night of camp," Joanne announced. "Tomorrow morning you go back home."

The kids gave a few sad groans.

"So there'll be a wild party in the Roaring Rec Room tonight," Joanne went on. "Wild as in animals, of course!"

Everyone cheered except for Nancy. The last day of camp meant they had only one day left to solve their case.

Her thoughts were interrupted by a loud yawn. She looked across the table and saw Marnie covering her mouth.

"Were you up again last night, Marnie?" Nancy asked.

"I guess," said Marnie. "Um . . . Vinnie snores."

"You've hardly slept since you came to camp!" Bess pointed out. "Maybe you should count sheep."

"Or lions or giraffes," George joked. "This is a zoo!"

Counting sheep made Nancy remember the creaky door. She was counting sheep the night she heard it.

"You guys," Nancy whispered, "do you think Marnie has been sneaking out at night?"

"You mean to steal the enrichment toys?" Bess asked.

"No way, Nancy," whispered George. "Marnie wants to be vet, not a thief!"

"I guess you're right," Nancy said. She closed her penguin pad and finished her waffles. Right after breakfast it was time for everybody's last zoo jobs.

"Nancy, Bess, and George," Joanne called. "It's your turn to tidy up the petting zoo."

"I know!" said Bess, lifting her foot. "I wore my pink rubber boots with the daisy design just for the occasion!"

"Give me a break," George groaned.

The girls walked together to the petting zoo, opened the white picket fence, and stepped inside. A zookeeper named Amy was in charge of the petting zoo that day. After showing off her giraffe-shaped earrings, she led them to the toolshed. Inside were rakes, shovels, and feed buckets.

Nancy pointed to a bag on the floor. Across it were the words PLASTER OF PARIS. "What's that, Amy?" she asked.

"That's quick-drying cement you mix with water," Amy explained. "We use it to repair cracks in the animals' houses."

"Can I do that?" asked Bess. "I love to fix things."

"Sure," Amy said. She grabbed two rakes and handed them to Nancy and George. "You two can work with these."

"What do we do?" George asked.

"Make sure the hay is evenly distributed on the ground," Amy explained. She nodded toward a row of buckets. "Then sprinkle some feed to the chickens."

Amy mixed water in a bucket for Bess's plaster of Paris. George raked the hay near the donkey barn. Nancy did the same near the lamb pen. She had to stop when two baby lambs scooted around her legs.

"Hey, Nancy, Bess!" George called. "Check it out!"

Nancy turned. George was holding her rake in one hand and pointing to the ground with the other.

"What did you find, George?" Bess asked as she and Nancy walked over. "Something gross?"

"Something *weird*!" George exclaimed.

Nancy looked down. Pressed into the mud were the strangest-looking footprints she had ever seen. They had long, curved toes, with the big toe pointed away from the others.

"Whoa!" Nancy gasped. "Where did those come from?"

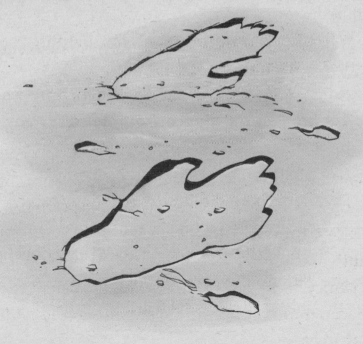

ChAPTER EighT

Party Snoopers

The girls stared down at the weird footprints.

"Those feet don't look human," Bess murmured.

"Or like any animal's in the petting zoo, either," said George. "Scary!"

Nancy glanced over her shoulder. Amy was trying to stop an alpaca from eating a boy's cap.

"Let's follow the trail!" Nancy suggested.

The footprints led all the way to the fence.

"Whoever these belong to must have climbed over the fence," Nancy decided. "That's how he or she got into the petting zoo."

"He, she, or *it*!" Bess added.

"Toys were stolen from the petting zoo," George said. "Do you think these footprints have anything to do with our case?"

"I'm not sure," Nancy replied. "But I wish there was a way we could save one footprint as a clue."

"There is!" said Bess. She kneeled down and began pouring the goopy plaster all over the footprint.

"Bess, what are you doing?" George asked.

"Amy said it's quick-drying cement," Bess explained.

"All we do now is wait until it dries, than dig it out."

"And we have a plaster cast!" Nancy said cheerily. "Way to go, Bess!"

Bess scooped the last drop of plaster out of the bucket, then turned the bucket over the footprint to protect it.

"Done!" she said. "We'll just pick it up after it dries."

"Nancy, Bess, George," Amy called across the

petting zoo. "Have you fed the chickens yet?"

The girls ran for buckets of feed. They opened the short fence surrounding the chicken coop and stepped inside. The clucking chickens hurried over as the girls sprinkled feed on the ground.

"They're hungrier than Vinnie!" George laughed.

"Heard that!" Vinnie's voice said.

He walked over clutching a cardboard box.

"Aren't you supposed to be making enrichment toys?" asked Nancy.

"What do you think these are?" Vinnie said with a smile. "Look what I made for the gophers and groundhogs!"

Vinnie reached into the box and pulled out a clear plastic ball. Inside the ball was a bright green jelly bean.

"The jelly beans are from my own stash," Vinnie said.

"What do the toys do?" Bess asked.

"They're Beany Balls," Vinnie explained.

"The jelly beans will rattle when the small animals roll them."

"Sweet!" said Nancy. Leave it to Vinnie to build a toy with candy inside!

"I just hope nobody steals them tonight." Vinnie sighed. He looked worried as he walked to the gopher house.

Nancy was worried too. They had no more suspects and no good clues. Just some weird-looking footprints in the mud!

"This is the wildest party ever!" George declared that night.

The Roaring Rec Room was decorated with tons of animal-print balloons. The campers wore animal masks they'd made that afternoon.

Nancy loved her giraffe mask with the crepe-paper eyelashes. Bess was stylin' in her glittery pink bear mask. George had made a lion mask with pipe-cleaner whiskers.

"How are we supposed to eat with these

things on?" Vinnie complained behind his eagle mask.

"Just *wing* it!" George joked.

The campers rocked out to some great music blaring from Ron's CD player.

"What's a zoo party without animal dances?" a zookeeper named Charlie announced. He taught the campers how to dance the Monkey, the Pony, and the Chicken Dance.

Abby danced over to Nancy, Bess, and George. Her sheep mask was made out of fluffy white cotton balls.

"You can't be such great detectives," Abby yelled over the music. "You never found out who took the missing toys!"

The girls rolled their eyes as Abby danced away.

"Blah, blah, blah," muttered George.

"You mean baa, baa, baa!" Bess giggled.

But Nancy wasn't laughing. "What if we are bad detectives, like Abby said?" she asked. "It's our last day of camp and we never found out what happened to the toys!"

"The day's not over yet!" George reminded her.

"You guys, what happened to Marnie?" said Bess, looking around the rec room. "She was here when the party started, but I haven't seen her since."

"Marnie was really tired today," Nancy said. "Let's find her and see if she's okay."

The music was still pumping as the girls left

the Roaring Rec Room. As they walked through the zoo, Nancy saw someone running in the distance. She squinted through the darkness.

"Marnie!" Nancy exclaimed.

"Where's she going?" asked Bess.

The three girls followed Marnie through the zoo. After making a sharp turn behind the Butterfly House, Marnie sprinted straight toward the Panda Bamboo Forest.

"Pandas?" George said. "What does she want with the pandas?"

Marnie darted across the bridge that led to the forest. She stopped in front of a tall metal shed and grabbed the handles. Then she began pulling at the doors.

"Phooey! Phooey! Phooey!" Marnie said. Her horse mask rested on top of her head as she kept tugging at the door handles.

"Bess, George!" Nancy gasped. "She's trying to open the pandas' toy cabinet!"

CHAPTER NINE

What's Up, Doc?

The girls scampered across the bridge, calling Marnie's name. Marnie spun around with wide eyes.

"Hi!" she blurted. "What's up?"

"Why aren't you at the party, Marnie?" asked George. "Chicken Dance not working out?"

"I need a Frisbee!" Marnie

said. She tugged at the doors again. "But the cabinet is locked!"

"Why do you need a Frisbee?" Nancy asked.

Marnie froze and said, "Um . . . for my costume."

Bess pointed to the mask on Marnie's head. "I know dogs catch Frisbees," she said. "Since when do horses?"

"What's the real reason, Marnie?" asked Nancy.

"It's a secret," Marnie said quickly.

"Is the secret that you've been stealing the animals' enrichment toys?" George asked.

"No!" Marnie cried. "I wanted to borrow a Frisbee for a sick animal in the hospital. She needs cheering up."

"Is she a panda?" Nancy asked.

Marnie shook her head. "There was a panda in the hospital last night," she said. "The night before, the vets treated a baby elephant with a splinter in his foot."

"How do you know?" asked Nancy.

"I was there!" Marnie replied. "I sneaked out both nights to the animal hospital."

Nancy stared at Marnie.

It *was* Marnie she had heard sneaking out!

"You took the enrichment toys so you could give them to the sick animals?" Nancy asked.

Marnie shook her head back and forth. "I only need a toy tonight," she said. "The other nights I just wanted to watch the vets."

"The vets let you?" Nancy asked, surprised. "Didn't they know you were supposed to be in the Discovery Den?"

"I sort of lied." Marnie sighed. "I told them Joanne said it was okay because I want to be a vet someday."

"Veterinarians are smart, Marnie," said Nancy. "Sneaking out in the middle of the night by yourself is pretty dumb."

"So was lying to the vets," Bess added.

Marnie cast her eyes downward. Nancy could tell she was sorry.

"You could use some strawberry lemonade,

Marnie," Nancy said with a smile. "Let's go back to the party and—"

"No!" Marnie said. "I have to see how Coconut is doing!"

"Who's Coconut?" George wondered.

"She's the chimp who swallowed something dangerous," Marnie explained. "Come on! See for yourself!"

Marnie raced ahead toward the hospital. Nancy, Bess, and George followed a few feet behind.

"Marnie still could have taken the toys," George whispered. "If she lied to the vets, how do we know she's not lying to us?"

They reached the hospital and charged through the front door. Petula was standing in the hallway, wringing her hands nervously. Dr. Vickers, the head veterinarian, was holding an X-ray up to the light.

"Coconut is very lucky, Petula," said Dr. Vickers. "The ball she swallowed didn't get stuck in her throat."

"Thank goodness!" Petula sighed in relief.

"How did Coconut get such a tiny toy ball?" Dr. Vickers asked. "I know you're very careful about what your chimps get their hands on."

"Children were visiting the Chimp Compound the other day." Petula sighed again. "One of them must have given the ball to Coconut."

Nancy couldn't imagine her fellow campers hurting any animals. Not even Abby, Brian, and Antonio!

"Dr. Vickers, may I please see that X-ray?" Marnie asked.

"Here, Marnie," Dr. Vickers said. She handed the X-ray over. "When you become a vet, you'll see many of these!"

Nancy, Bess, and George peered over Marnie's shoulders as she studied Coconut's X-ray.

"See?" Marnie said, pointing to the X-ray. "You can see the little ball right there in her stomach."

"There's something inside the ball," Nancy

pointed out. "Something shaped like a jelly bean."

"The Beany Ball!" Bess gasped. "Vinnie left those little balls in the petting zoo for the smaller animals."

The wheels inside Nancy's head began to spin. The petting zoo was where they found those weird footprints!

"Maybe those weird footprints belonged to *chimps!*" Nancy blurted.

"Chimps?" asked George.

"The blue cotton candy Ambrose ate was outside the Chimp Compound," Nancy explained. "So was the Beany Ball."

"So was that banana peel!" Bess pointed out.

"But Petula says her chimps don't leave the compound," Marnie said. "They'd have to break out—but how?"

Nancy studied Petula as she thought. Her chimps weren't just any chimps. They learned human skills.

"You guys," Nancy said slowly, "maybe the chimps in the compound didn't *have* to break out."

CHAPTER TEN

Chimpan-See!

Bess, George, and Marnie stared at Nancy as if she were from outer space.

"Petula said that her chimps learned how to lock and unlock a door," Nancy began explaining. "They could have unlocked the door and let themselves out."

"Omigosh!" said Marnie. "Ambrose opened a door here yesterday. We saw it with our own eyes!"

The girls spun around when they heard a rattling noise. A vet was wheeling a gurney down the hall. Lying on it was a chimp, half covered with a sheet.

"Coconut!" Petula cried. She ran to the chimp

and stroked her hairy forehead. "I won't let anyone give you dangerous toys again."

"Hooooo," Coconut cooed.

The girls stared at Coconut's feet wiggling out from underneath the sheet.

"I'll be right back!" George said.

"Where are you going?" asked Nancy.

George didn't answer as she shot out of the hospital. A few minutes later she was back with the plaster cast.

When Petula turned away, George ran straight to the gurney. She placed it next to Coconut's foot and said, "A perfect match!"

"That proves that a chimp was in the petting zoo," Nancy said with a smile. "And if a chimp can be in the petting zoo, he or she can be *anywhere* in the zoo!"

"Do you think they had something to do with the missing toys?" Bess asked.

"There's one way to find out," Nancy said. "Let's check out the Chimp Compound!"

Nancy, Bess, George, and Marnie raced out of the hospital to the Chimp Compound. The front door was locked.

The girls scurried around to find a back door. But as they walked through tall grass Nancy heard a noise.

CRUNCH!

"What was that?" Marnie asked.

Nancy looked down. She kicked aside the blades of grass and gasped. Scattered on the ground were toys. But not just any toys. There were rope toys, cardboard tube toys, even a boomer ball!

"Enrichment toys!" Nancy exclaimed. "The

chimps must have taken them and hidden them back here!"

"How come Petula didn't know?" George wondered.

Nancy pointed out the long grass. "It looks like nobody ever comes back here," she said. "Even Petula!"

"Hoo-hoo-hoooo!"

The back door suddenly swung open. Nancy's jaw dropped as an army of chimps filed out of the building.

"Hey!" Marnie shouted to the chimps. "Where do you think you're going?"

The chimps scampered away from the compound into the zoo. Some chimps grinned with big white teeth. Others grabbed enrichment toys on their way, waving them in the air.

"They might swallow more toys!" Bess said.

"Or eat more cotton candy!" George said.

"We have to stop them!" Nancy declared.

The girls stampeded after the chimps. But

just as they were gaining on them, Joanne jumped in their path.

"There you are!" Joanne said. "I thought I told you girls not to run off without telling me."

Ron came running over. So did the other campers. Some were still wearing their masks.

"Sorry we ran off," Nancy said. She pointed at the chimps. "But now the chimpanzees are on the run!"

"Chimpanzees?" Joanne said.

Ron looked at the chimps charging into the zoo. "Cheese and crackers!" he cried. "How are we going to catch them?"

"Here I come to save the day!" a voice cried out.

Out of the darkness stepped Ethan. He was smiling and holding a bunch of banana peels strung together.

"Ethan, what is that goofy gizmo?" Ron asked.

"It's my latest invention, the Furbisher Chimp-Rope!" Ethan explained. "The first jump rope made out of banana peels!"

"Not again!" Ron groaned.

Ethan held up his invention. Then he shouted in the direction of the chimps, "Hey, guys! Who wants to play?"

The chimps stopped. Their eyes lit up in the dark and they began to screech. In a flash the runaway chimps were charging toward Ethan.

"Hoo-hoo-hoo!" they hooted.

Everyone laughed as the chimps swung and tugged the banana jump rope.

"Well, what do you know?" Ron said. "It worked!"

Petula came running over.

"I thought I heard my chimps," Petula said. She twisted her hands nervously. "What are they doing outside?"

"The chimps used their door-opening skills to leave the compound at night," Nancy explained.

"And they came back with toys," Bess said. "Our enrichment toys."

Surprised voices filled the air.

"How did they know there were toys out there?" Joanne asked.

"They probably found some on their first night out," Nancy said. "After that, they couldn't get enough of them."

"I see," Petula said slowly. "Then the special Project Primate learning toys didn't work out."

"Neither did Project Wildebeest," Ron wailed. "It was a failure. A total failure!"

Nancy felt badly for Ron. "Excuse me, Mr. Furbisher," she said. "But maybe you don't really need Project Wildebeest."

All eyes turned to Nancy.

"What?" Ron gasped.

"Instead of us teaching the animals what we want," Nancy suggested with a smile, "why don't we let the animals teach us what *they* want?"

Ron stared at Nancy. Then he scratched his chin thoughtfully. "I like it . . . I like it," he said slowly. "We can call it Project—"

"Chimpanzee!" Petula cut in excitedly.

The campers giggled as Petula and Ron exchanged a high five.

"Okay, kids," said Joanne. "Let's help Petula pick up these toys."

"Then it's back to the party!" Vinnie cheered.

The campers spread out to pick up the toys. Abby walked over to Nancy, Bess, and George. She smiled apologetically.

"I guess you guys are pretty good detectives,"

Abby admitted. "So forget everything I said, okay?"

"Okay," Nancy said. She glanced at the chimps frolicking with the banana jump rope. "But I am never, ever going to forget this case!"

The next morning the campers packed up to go home. After a good-bye breakfast, they were all given their zookeeper badges. Then Petula made a special announcement.

"I've decided that fun toys for the chimps aren't a bad idea after all," Petula said. "So it's Frisbees and jump ropes all around!"

Nancy and her fellow campers cheered loudly.

"And *I've* decided to let Ethan make those toys!" Ron added. He raised an eyebrow at his son. "As long as he promises to stop swimming in the seal pond!"

"Deal," Ethan said with a grin.

Nancy, Bess, and George smiled. Now that they'd solved the case, they were really happy campers. And they still loved animals—more than ever!

"I wonder if we can be zookeepers *and* detectives," Bess said dreamily.

"Sure!" said Nancy. She swung her arms around both friends' shoulders. "We'll just call ourselves . . . the Zoo Crew!"

Amazing animal cards!

Your BFFs will go wild when they open up an amazing animal card—made by you!

You Will Need:

Construction paper or heavier card stock

Scissors

Markers or crayons

A ruler

Plastic googly eyes

Glue

The Rules:

❀ Fold paper in half.

❀ Draw an outline of your favorite animal on

one side of the folded paper. Make sure to draw the top part of the head or tail at least one quarter of an inch from the fold. (Measure with your ruler to be sure.)

❀ Use scissors to cut out your animal. Be super careful not to cut the top parts along the fold. This will connect the front part of the card to the back.

❀ Face it! What's an animal without creature-features? Grab your markers or crayons and draw your animal a face. Then glue on the googly eyes for extra fun!

❀ Add the finishing touch: zebra stripes, leopard spots, elephant wrinkles—or go glam with glitter!

❀ Open your card and write an animal-friendly message: Get well-ephant! Happy grrr-day! Best friends fur-ever! Sealed with a kiss!

You're done! But remember, don't stop with just one animal or two: Get crafty and make a whole zoo!

What happens when a bunch
of kids take over a forgotten
little garden plot?

the
FRIENDSHIP
garden